LITTLE

FRAN

CHAPTER I

A quaint old Japanese garden lay smiling under the sunshine of a morning in early spring. The sun, having flooded the outside world with dazzling light, seemed to sink to a tender radiance as it wooed leaf and bud into new life and loveliness. It loosened the tiny rivulet from the icy fingers of winter, and sped it merrily on its way to a miniature lake, where shining goldfish darted here and there in an ecstasy of motion. It stole into the shadows of a great pine-tree, and touched the white wings of the pigeons as they cooed the song of mating-time. It gleamed on the sandy path that led to the old stone lantern, played into the eyes of Kwannon, the Goddess of Mercy, and finally lost itself in the trees beyond.

Under a gnarled plum-tree, that for uncounted years had braved the snow and answered joyously the first call of spring, a little maiden stood and held out eager hands to catch the falling blossoms. The flowering-time was nearly done, and the child stood watching the petals twirl quickly down, filling the hollows and fashioning curious designs on the mossy grass.

The softest of breezes coming across the river, over the thick hedge, saucily blew a stray petal straight into the child's face. To Yuki Chan it was a challenge, and with outstretched hands and flying feet she gave chase to the whirling blossoms. Round and round the old tree, into the hedge, and up the sandy path she raced, her long sleeves spreading like tiny sails, her cheeks flushed to the same crimson as her flowery playmates. A sudden stillness in the air ended the romp. Yuki Chan returned to her playground beneath the tree, and taking her captured petals from the folds of her kimono, began to count her trophies.

"Ichi, ni, san, ichi, ni, san," she rhythmically droned, three being the magical number that would bring good luck if the petals were properly arranged and the number repeated often enough.

But the monotony of repetition brought rest, and soon Yuki Chan, forgetting to count, made a bed of the fallen petals and turned her face toward the little straw-roofed house from which noises of busy preparation came.

It was a birthday. Not Yuki Chan's, for that came with the snow-time. This was the third day of the third month, which in the long ago was set apart as the big birthday of all little girls born in the lovely island, and was celebrated by the Festival of Dolls.

Yuki Chan lay with her slim body stretched in the warmth of the sun. In every graceful line was the imprint of high breeding; her white face, so unusual with her race, was stamped with the romance and tragedy of centuries; while her eyes, limpid and luminous, looked out at the world with eager, questioning interest.

Through the wide-open *shoji* of the house she caught glimpses of her father and mother hurrying and holding consultations. She marked frequent visits to the old warehouse that held the household treasures, and the bringing out of bundles wrapped in yellow cloth. The air brought her whiffs of cooking food, and the flower- and fish- men deposited a fair part of their stock on the porch. But Yuki Chan was banished from these joys of preparation because of naughtiness, and as she lay in the warm sunshine she thought of her recent wickedness. She smiled as she remembered how she had hid her father's pipe that he might work the faster, and broken the straps of her mother's wooden shoes, so that she could not go outdoors. She laughed softly when she thought of the stray cat which she had brought into the house and coaxed to drink milk while she, with skilful fingers and a pair of scissors, transformed her smooth fur into a wonderful landscape garden. Short work had made kitty's head slick and shiny, like a lake, with a stray bristle or two, which stood for trees. In the middle of her back stood Fuji, the great mountain, with numberless little Fujis to keep company. Many winding paths ran down kitty's legs to queer, shapeless shrines, and it was only when Yuki Chan had insisted on making a curious old pine-tree with twisted limbs of kitty's short and stubby tail that trouble ensued, and she had been requested by her mother to take her honorable little body to the garden.

Yuki Chan remembered her mother's beautiful smile of love as she gently chided her, and recalled the note of trouble in the kind voice. Was the mother sorry because she had stuck out a very pink tongue at a cross-eyed old image that sat on the floor on the very spot that she wanted to step upon? Or was it—and Yuki Chan grew grave—that the last *go rin* had been spent for the new dress she was to wear that day?

All her short life Yuki Chan had lived in a house of love, but no veil of affection, no sacrifice, could shield her from the knowledge of poverty. She had never seen her mother wear but one festival dress, yet her own little kimono was ever bright and dainty, and even the new brocade of the dolls' dresses stood alone with the weave of gold and tinsel.

A solemn thought, like a pebble dropped into water, caused circle after circle to trouble her childish mind. She did not quite understand, but she knew there was something she must learn. She had been naughty and weighed her mother's spirits. She had caused a grave look in her father's kind eyes, and had sent the household pets scattering with her mischief. Now she must be good—very good—else the fox spirit would come upon her, and she would go through life an unhappy soul. She would give more obedience to the honorable mother, whose every word had been a caress. It was as if for the first time the great book of life opened before her and, though unconscious of its meaning, the first word she saw spelled Duty.

The noises from the house grew fainter. The child, with blinking eyes, lay gazing straight above her. Overhead the branches overflowed into a canopy of crimson, which shut out the great real world and opened into a fairy world wherein only the untried feet of youth may tread and the fragile flowers of child-dreams bloom. The gates thereto are slight but strong, and only knowledge erects an impassable barrier.

The wind sang its lullaby through the blossoms of the tree, and sleep would soon have overtaken Yuki Chan had not a peculiar sound aroused her and caused her eyes to fly wide open. Once before she had heard it, and it had meant death to the big robin who lived in the branches above. The cry came from the mother bird this time and brought Yuki Chan to her feet.

Through the shower of blossoms, brought down by the mad fluttering of wings, she saw a tiny half-feathered thing struggling in the sharp claws of her lately acquired pet. With certainty of success, the cat let its victim weakly flutter an inch or two away, then reaching out a cruel paw drew it back. Twice repeated, the green eyes narrowed to slits, and Yuki Chan, horrified, saw big red drops slowly dripping from either side of the whiskered mouth. Terror held her for a moment as she heard the crunching of small bones, then white passion enveloped her as she stole noiselessly from behind and closed her two small hands around the furry throat.

"*Baka!*" she cried from between her clenched teeth. "*Baka*—to eat the baby birds! This day will I ask Oni to make you into a stone, which every foot will kick and hurt, and you can neither move nor cry. You cruel, cruel beast!" In vain the cat struggled. Yuki Chan held it firmly at arm's-length while she decided what was to be its fate.

Looking sternly at the offender, her lips rounded into a long-drawn "s-o," the light of anticipated revenge danced in her eyes. At last she knew what to do, O most honorable but very ugly cat! She would throw her into the ditch, where great crawling frogs with popping eyes would stick out long tongues; where flying things would sting, and creeping things would bite; where the great tide would come later and take her out to the big, big ocean, where there was neither milk to drink nor birds to eat.

At the thought of her furry playmate floating alone and hungry in the vast place which, to Yuki Chan, had neither beginning nor end, something of pity touched her heart, and she slightly loosened her grasp.

The cat gained a good breath and used it. In the fight for freedom a sharp claw was drawn down the child's arm, leaving a line of red in its course. Compassion took flight, and Yuki Chan, clutching anew, went swiftly down the path that led to the street, with a watchful eye on the lodge of the keeper of the gate.

The keeper was very old, and very cross, and lately had acquired a curious idea that little girls must ask his honorable permission to go in and out the gate. One day he actually threatened punishment, and Yuki Chan, in her scorn, invited him to cut off his head with a sword, that he might save his face. Now the way was clear.

She turned her head and bumped her small body against the weight of the heavy gates until they swung slightly apart and permitted her to slip through.

So intent was her purpose to reach the ditch across the street that she did not see an approaching jinrikisha, and before she knew it she had been tumbled over and sent rolling to the side of the road. Still clutching the kitten, she sat up and rubbed the dust from her eyes.

Standing over her was the jinrikisha man, and beside him was his passenger, a young American boy, whose light hair and blue eyes held her spell-bound. He was brushing the dust from her kimono, and his foreign tongue made strange sounds.

"Say, kid," the boy was saying, as he transferred the dust from his hands to his handkerchief, "glad you're not hurt or got any bones cracked. Where's your mama, or your papa, or your nurse, to give you a spanking and keep you off the street?"

As he talked Yuki Chan grew fascinated watching his mouth, and forgot, for a moment, her direful intention. The cat, again taking advantage of her relaxed hold, began to tug for freedom, and a lively struggle ensued.

The boy, looking on, began to laugh, a laugh that began in his eyes, ran over his face and down into his throat, whence it came again in a shout of boyish merriment.

Yuki Chan, looking from him to the smiling jinrikisha man, grew crimson with anger. With a swift movement she ran toward the ditch.

Divining her purpose by the look in her eyes, Dick Merrit went gallantly to the rescue of the kitten. He was tall for his sixteen years, and his long strides more than matched the pattering steps of the slip of a girl who raced before him.

"No, you don't, kiddie," he cried; "your manicured cat is not going into the ditch, if we have to scrap for it."

Merrit caught Yuki Chan in one arm, and again and again loosened her fingers from the struggling kitten.

"Iya, Iya!" the child screamed; but Merrit, as determined as she, held her firmly, and ended by lightly slapping first one little hand and then the other.

The child, thus coming into contact for the first time with physical force, relaxed her grasp and gazed in amazement at the boy's determined face.

"I guess your 'Iya' means no, little lady, and I say 'Iya' too," said Merrit, taking the cat into his arms and smoothing its uneven back. "You are not going to put it into the ditch. Why don't you give it to me? I am getting up a collection of cats and things at the school, and I'd like to take this queer specimen along. Ask her if I can have it."

The jinrikisha man, who stood a smiling spectator, saw Dick Merrit's hand move toward his pocket, and was instantly alert and eager to settle the matter.

"Him ve'y bad girl," he said; "him make dead for catty. You give me ten sen, I take girl homely. You have much of catty."

But Dick declined all interference, and putting the cat inside his coat he stooped down and took one of Yuki Chan's unresisting hands. Her sleeve fell back, and he saw the long red scratch.

"Hello! The cat had an inning too, didn't she? I'd like to chuck her for hurting you, but I can't let you give her a bath in that dirty hole. Never mind, I'll take her home, and some day I'll bring you something. I bet you don't understand a word I'm saying, but I'll be hanged if I know how to make you."

Feeling rather helpless, Dick talked on, patting first Yuki Chan and then the cat.

The child stood speechless and looked deep into his eyes, not having entirely recovered from the shock of the first blow she had ever received.

"You'll be good, won't you?" he went on coaxingly, "not drown any more cats and things?"

Yuki Chan, with the intuition that only a child can have, suddenly bridged the gulf of strange language and understood. With the quick movement of a nestling bird, she bent forward and laid her cheek against the boy's shoulder. It was not only complete surrender, but allegiance to the conqueror.

Dick rose, red and confused. Then he climbed into the jinrikisha, trying to ignore the smiles of the man.

Yuki Chan, with her hands joined just below her sash, bent her body like a half-shut jack-knife.

"Arigato—arigato," she said politely, as she bowed again and again.

"Him say t'ank you," interpreted the jinrikisha man.

"Good-by," called Dick. "Don't forget—be good!"

Yuki Chan watched the back of the jinrikisha and the swinging brown legs of the jinrikisha man that showed beneath. She had forgotten the cat, but she still remembered the kind look in the blue eyes of the boy.

"Yuki, Yuki!" came the voice of the mother in her native tongue. "Come, the feast is prepared, and the sandals are worn from my feet running to seek you. Hurry! before the red beans grow cold."

The child sent a long-drawn "Hei" in answer to her mother, then to herself she said over and over:

"Be goodu—be goodu."

She had heard the words a few times before, but they were associated with her visits to the mission-school and a certain oblong box out of which came sticks of red and white with a very sweet taste. Now, as she said them, a new meaning seemed to play about them.

She slipped through the gate and walked with unhurried feet toward the small house, so gay in its festal plumage. As she passed the old plum- tree she looked up and saw the mother bird cuddling her babies beneath her breast.

Some tender thought lighted the child's face into a strange beauty, as a stray sunbeam finds a hidden flower and glorifies it. Turning her face upward to the nest, she patted her own cheek and said: "Be goodu, Yuki, be goodu."

CHAPTER II

In the springtime a Japanese house is a fairy-like thing, with only top and bottom of straw and a few upholding posts to give it a look of substance.

Yuki Chan's house was typical. The paper screens were carefully put away during the day, that the breezes might play unobstructed through the house. At night the heavy wooden doors were fitted into grooves and served not only to keep out the night air, but also the evil spirits that come abroad when the great sun ceases watching.

Binding the whole was a narrow porch, showing a floor polished like a mirror from the slipping and sliding of generations of feet. Yuki Chan first learned to know her face in its reflections and, alas! by the same method had learned the saucy fascination of sticking out her small pink tongue.

On the side of the porch toward the plum-tree the child found her father and mother waiting. The two old people sat on gay cushions with hands folded and feet crossed. Their festal attire bore the marks of a once careless luxury, but now shabbiness tried to hide itself under the bravery of tinsel, where once had been pure gold.

Each year the struggle of obsolete methods of business and the intricacies of progress plowed the furrows a little deeper in the man's face, and when his eyes, that in youth had blazed with ambition, grew wistful and troubled, he dropped them that his wife might not see.

But what silence could hide from this frail woman any mood of the man she had served with mind and body and soul these many years? When she came to him as a shy bride on trial, she knew no such word as love. Duty was her entire vocabulary, and she asked nothing and gave all.

Many little souls had come to her, with hands all crimped and pink, like new-blown cherry-leaves, only to close their eyes and pass out to the good god Jizo, who is always waiting to help little children across the river of death.

In years gone by, night after night sleep had flown before the terror that another woman would be brought into the house that the family name might not die out. Silently she would slip out to the little shrine and pour out passionate words of prayer that just one little soul might be permitted to live.

No matter how long the night, nor how bitter the struggle, morning always found her bright and cheerful, bending every effort to invent new diversions for her husband. She labored to anticipate every wish, and even though she did without, she provided him the best of comfort. Working far into the night, secretly disposing of her small personal treasures, acquiescing in his most trivial statements, she planned that no slightest gap in the domestic arrangement should suggest itself to him.

The woman worked and prayed and waited. Then she triumphed. In the wake of a great snow-storm came the longed-for child, and they called her Yuki, after the snow that had brought them their wish. Hand in hand with Yuki Chan came love, and bound the hearts of the man and woman with ties of a desire fulfilled. From that time to this love had prevailed, and as Yuki Chan climbed on the porch, besmirching its shining surface with her muddy little feet, that had been guiltless of sandals all day, the faces of the two old people lighted up with sudden joy.

Yuki Chan looked ruefully at the muddy prints she had made and realized that she had been a most impolite little girl. Remembering her recent resolve, she sought the eyes in which she had never seen any light for her save that of love. She drew close, and reaching down took her mother's hand, hard and cracked by labor, and laying her cheek against it said, with a voice sure of forgiveness and sweet desire for atonement:

"Go men nasai."

The mother, with a courtly but playful air, granted her pardon with a low salutation. Then with a rush of affection that no convention could stem, she folded the child to her heart and lived another moment of supreme joy.

The father sat by, making no comment, his eyes bright and twinkling. Then he suggested that their Majesties, the dolls, had been waiting long on the shelf. Was it not time they were receiving a visit?

The years of toil were telling on both father and mother, but they daily refreshed themselves at the overbrimming fountain of Yuki Chan's youth, and now, as they each took one of her hands to go in to see the dolls, they were so gay that the child suggested that instead of walking they should do the new one-two-three-hop she had learned at the kindergarten.

It was unheard-of conduct, but it was for Yuki Chan, and father and mother stumped along, cheered on by the small girl who was trying to keep time, but was breathless through sheer excess of happiness.

There was nothing in the room to impede their progress. No chairs with treacherous legs to trip over, no beds, nor tables with sharp corners —nothing whatever but the matting, soft and thick, where Yuki Chan had practised all the gymnastics of childhood unbruised and unharmed.

Half skipping, half hopping, and wholly undone with laughter and exertion, the three at last reached the place where, for six years, offerings had been made for the gift of the child who stood to these two for love.

Arranged in the best room in the house, on five long red-covered shelves, were dolls. Big dolls and little dolls, thin ones and fat ones, each one to represent some royal man or woman of the long ago, and dressed in a fashion of a time almost forgotten. There was Jimmu Tenno, the first real emperor. His hair was done in a curious fashion and his dress was of a wonderful brocade, while his hands clasped two fierce-looking swords. There was Jingo, too, who had won fame and lasting honor by her wonderful fighting, and was so great she had to sit by the emperors and look down on the other empresses. Such a lot of them! Some worthy to be remembered every day in the year, others the more quickly forgotten the better.

Yuki Chan knew them all by heart, and she lingered before those she liked and quickly passed those she did not care for. She could not be rude to an emperor, even though he had been dead hundreds of years. She was really not very afraid of the greatness of the old doll men and women who sat on the shelf, still it was well to be careful about handling them. She might be turned into a lizard or a snake, just as the old lodge-keeper had said.

But her delight was in the miniature toilet articles of solid silver, costly gold lacquer, and porcelain, so tiny, so beautifully carved they must have meant the eyesight of some workman, only too glad to shut out the sunlight forever if he might produce just one perfect thing.

The things, however, that made Yuki Chan clap her hands and the nesting birds perk up their heads at the sound of her clear, sweet laugh were the funny little lacquer carts in which the royalty was supposed to ride, drawn by impossible fat bullocks, so bow-legged that their curves formed a big round O. Yuki Chan made her red lips into the same shape, and called her mother to look.

She pretended to feed the dolls with real food and wine, and actually played with the five court musicians, because they were partly servants and it did not matter.

Her tongue ran in ceaseless chatter. Her father and mother hovered around her, repeating the history of all those wonderful people. Yuki Chan listened very little, so concerned was she with her own comments, until she happened to see an anxious look creep into her mother's eyes. It was something every little girl must know, and if Yuki Chan's honorable ears refused to open, how would she learn? Then Yuki Chan nestled close, and gave little pats of love and tried to listen. THE shadows of the bamboo grew long and slim as the sun kissed them good night. The sails skimmed homeward on a silver sea as the west covered its rosy pink in a veil of deepest blue. The young birds in the old plum-tree did not stir at the loving touch of the mother who, with a soft bill, searched and sought for the lost one. The plum-blossoms lingered yet for a night as the air had grown chill.

Within the house Yuki Chan, still dressed, lay on the floor, weary with the wonders of the day. Her mother took from a small inclosure beneath a shelf many soft comforts with which she arranged the child's bed. Yuki Chan, talking all the time in a low monotone, tried to unravel a tangle in her mind of birds and cats and dolls. It was all getting unmanageable and very hazy, when her mother gathered her into her arms, and quickly casting aside her two garments laid her gently in a bath of caressing warmth. A moment more and the little maiden lay like a rose-leaf in her bed.

The night-lamp made shadowy ghosts of all it touched, and one gleam of light, escaping the paper shade, hung like an aureole above the head of Yuki Chan's mother as she knelt with clasped hands before the Buddha on the shelf.

Her moving lips had only one refrain: "The child, the child, the child."

Yuki Chan watched the play of the light in the half-dark room. What funny things those shadows made, and, strangely enough, one more wonderful than all the rest grew into the shape of the boy, and his lips were saying, "Be good."

Then Yuki Chan lost herself in a mist of drowsiness, and her mother sat by, and kept time with her hand as she chanted rather than sang:

"Sleep, little one, sleep.
The sparrows are nodding.
Beneath the deep willow-trees
The night-lamp is burning.
Thy mother is watching,
Sleep, little one, sleep."

CHAPTER III

Twelve times had the plum-tree scattered its petals to the wind, and Yuki San [Footnote: The honorific *Chan*, used only in childhood, is changed to *San* in later years.] had passed from childhood into girlhood, and had already touched the border of that grave land of grown-up, where all the worries lie. For though she was apparently only a larger edition of the spoiled, impulsive happy child of old, yet often her eyes were shadowed with the struggle of shielding her aging father and mother from the poverty that was coming closer day by day.

During the three years she had been gaining her education at the English mission-school, they had toiled unceasingly that she might have the best the country could afford, but now that she had returned after her long struggle with a strange language and a strange people, it was but fitting that she should take up her duties as the daughter of an impoverished family of high rank. The father, grown old and feeble, gave up the battle for existence, and being a devout Buddhist, turned his thoughts upon Nirvana, which he strove diligently to enter by perpetual meditation and prayer. The mother, used to guidance and unable to think or plan for herself, turned helplessly to Yuki San.

The duties were heavy for girlish shoulders, and often as the dawn crept over the mountains it found the girl wide-eyed and still, trying to solve the problem of modest demand and meager supply.

She had learned many things at the mission-school. She could read and write English imperfectly, she could recite the multiplication table faster than any one else, she could perform the most intricate figures in physical culture, and if she had infinite time she could play three hymns on the organ. These varied accomplishments, however, seemed of little assistance in showing her how to stretch her father's small pension beyond the barest necessities of the household. Tales had been told her of a great land, far beyond her sea-bound home, where women of the highest birth went out to work in the busy world. How she had marveled at their boldness and wondered at the customs that would permit it! Now she half envied them their freedom, and sighed over the iron-bound etiquette that forbade a departure from her father's roof save for the inevitable end of all Japanese women—a prearranged marriage.

It was for this she had been so carefully trained in all phases of housekeeping, and in all the intricacies of social life. Her education from birth had been with a view of making smooth the path of her future husband that his home might be peaceful and he untroubled.

Each day as the burden grew heavier she fought her battle with the bravery and courage of youth. With jests and chatter she served her parents' simple meals, constantly urging them to further indulgence of what she pretended was a great feast, but which in reality she had secretly sacrificed some household treasure to obtain. She deftly turned the rice-bucket as she served, that they might not see the scant supply. With great ceremony she poured the hot water into the bowls, insisting that no other *sake* was made such as this. Her determination to keep them happy and ignorant of the true conditions taxed her every resource, but it was her duty, and duty to Yuki San was the only religion of which she was sure.

But one day a great event happened in the little home. Yuki San was called before her father and told, in ceremonious language, that a marriage had been arranged for her with Saito San, a wealthy officer in the Emperor's household. She laid her head upon the mats and gave thanks to the gods. Now her father and mother would live in luxury for the rest of their lives!

Saito San was to her only a far-away, shadowy being, whom she was to obey for the rest of her life and whose house she was to keep in order. He was a means to an end, and entered into her thoughts merely as one to whom she was deeply grateful. Youth and all its joys were strong within her, and the pressure of poverty gone, her whole nature rebounded with delight.

Many times had marriage been proposed for her, for the story of her beauty and obedience had spread, but her father guarded his treasure zealously, and it was not until an offer came, suiting his former rank and condition, that he gave his consent.

Now, when he saw the happy light in the eyes of his child, and saw the color come into her cheeks, he laid his hands upon her head and blessed her. When Yuki San was by herself she clapped her hands joyfully. "I make happy like 'Merican," she whispered. "Hooray, hooray! now my troublesome make absence," and she hurried away to put a thank-offering before the household god.

Having arranged all preliminaries and instructed the mother to sell every household treasure that his child's clothes might do honor to the rich man's house, the father went back once more to his pipe and his dreams.

Yuki San and her mother were up with the sun, sewing and embroidering, and going about their daily task with zest and song. The past trials were forgotten and the future not considered.

One morning, not many weeks after the marriage had been arranged, Yuki San heard the call of the *Yubin* San, and running out to meet him, received a strange-looking letter. The envelope was white and square, and straight across the middle, in very plain English, was her name and address. Puzzled, she turned it over and over, then broke the seal.

The picture of the big hotel at the top of the sheet was so distracting that for a time she could get no further, but a word here and there and the signature at the end finally made her cry out with delight and surprise.

"Oh! it's from that funny lil' boy what gave spank to my hands long time ago. He want to come to my house for stay. Listen."

There was no one to listen but her own happy self, and lying flat upon the floor she propped her glowing face between her palms, while she read aloud from the letter spread before her:

YOKOHAMA.
Miss YUKI INOUYE—
Dear Miss Inouye: I wonder if you remember an American boy with whom you had an encounter in your very early days, because he dared to thwart your plans concerning a cat? I remember it very well, and the jolly picnics and excursions that you and my mother and I took together afterward.

I hope you have not forgotten me, for I am going to claim the privilege of the conqueror in that old battle and ask a favor of you. My Government has sent me out to your country on some important business, and finding there was no hotel close to my work, I wrote to the school where my mother and I visited twelve years ago, and asked them to recommend a family that would be good enough to take me in for two months. Strangely enough your father's name was suggested, and when I read that the only daughter both spoke and wrote English, and that her name was Yuki San, my mind flew back to my "Little Sister Snow" of the days gone by.

Could your father manage to accommodate me for a couple of months, if I promise to be very good and take up as little room as possible? If you think he can, please wire me here at Yokohama, and I'll come straight down.

Hoping to see you very soon, I am
Your old friend,
RICHARD MELTON MERRIT.

Yuki San turned the letter this way and that, and vainly tried to decipher the strange words. It was undoubtedly English, but not the English she was used to. She ran for her small dictionary and diligently searched out the meaning of each phrase.

Yes, she remembered the boy—he had light hair, and blue eyes that laughed, and he was a big, big boy and carried her on his shoulder.

She sat with the folded letter clasped carefully in her hands and gave herself up to joyous anticipation. A foreign guest was coming to stay two whole months in her house; after that she was to be married and wear her beautiful kimono, and give rich gifts to her father and mother.

Surely Buddha was caring for her! There had been grave moments of doubt about it since she left the mission-school, for he had never seemed to listen, though she prayed him night and day. But he had been only waiting to send all her happiness at once—he was a good god, kind and thoughtful. To-morrow, before the sun touched the big pine- tree on the mountain-top, she would go to the temple and tell him so.

Yuki San's plans found favor with her parents, chiefly because of their great desire to give her pleasure, and incidentally because the board of the foreigner would swell the fund that was needed for her marriage.

The plighted maid to them was already the wife, and the danger of a youthful heart defying tradition and clearing the bars of conventionality to reach its own desire was something unknown to these simple people. The child wished the foreigner to come—they could give her few pleasures—she should have her desire.

The sending of the telegram was the first exciting thing to be attended to. Five times Yuki San rewrote the short message, finding her fingers less deft than her tongue in framing an English sentence. Gravely and with effort she wrote:

"I give you all my house. Your lovely friend, Yuki."

But she shook her head over this and tried again:

"You have the welcome of my heart. Yuki."

This, too, fell short of her ideal, so she decided to send simply two words of which she was quite sure:

"Please come."

The days that followed were crowded with busy preparation. The difficulty of providing the ease and comfort that the presence of so honorable a guest demanded taxed to the utmost Yuki San's resourceful nature. Gaily she set her wits and fingers to work—placing a heavy brass *hibachi* over a black scorch in the matting, fitting new rice- paper into the small wooden squares of the *shoji*, and hanging *kakemono* over the ugly holes made by the missing plaster in the wall.

From one part of the house to another she flitted, laughing and working, while the old garden echoed her happiness and overflowed with blossom and song.

On the day of Merrit's expected arrival, when the last flower had been put in the vases, and the last speck of dust flecked from the matting, Yuki San's keen eyes detected a torn place in the paper door which separated the guest-chamber from the narrow hall.

A puzzled little frown drew her black brows together, but it soon fled before her smile.

"Ah!" she cried, "idea come quickly! I write picture of bamboo on teared place."

With paint and brush she fell to work, and beneath her skilful fingers the ugly tear disappeared in a forest of slender *take* which stretched away to the foot of a snow-capped mountain.

With a last touch she sank back on her heels and viewed her work with deep satisfaction. "All finished," she said, opening wide her arms; "no more to do now but wait for that time 'Merican sensei call jollyful!"

A laugh behind her made her turn her head quickly, and there in the doorway stood a tall foreigner, with outstretched hand of welcome.

Hand-shaking was an unknown art with Yuki San, so after one startled upward glance she touched her head to the floor in gracious courtesy.

All her gay spirits and freedom of speech vanished, and she was instantly enveloped in a mist of shyness and reserve that Merrit's direct look did not serve to lessen.

With lowered eyes, she ushered him into the larger living-room, and bade him be seated and accept all the hospitality her father's poor house could give.

After a long and tiresome journey Merrit found something inexpressibly charming in the quiet, picturesque place, and in the silent young girl who sat so demurely in the shadow. He tactfully ignored her timidity by talking cheerful nonsense about impersonal things, treating her as a bashful child who wanted to be friends but hardly dared.

As he talked Yuki San gained courage, and ventured many curious glances at the broad-shouldered young fellow, whose figure seemed completely to fill the room. At first she saw only a strange foreigner, but gradually, as she watched his face and listened to his unfamiliar speech, she discovered a long-lost playmate.

Through all the years that she had struggled for an education at the mission-school, English had been invariably associated with a tall, awkward, foreign boy, whose mouth made funny curves and whose eyes laughed when he made strange sounds. How big and splendid and handsome he had grown! How different his clothes from any she had ever seen before! How white his long hands, whose strong, firm touch she remembered so well! She looked and looked again, drinking in the tones of his deep voice, till the throbbing of her heart sent a flood of crimson to her cheeks.

But gradually her shyness wore away, and when Merrit asked her how in the world he was to conduct his business with so few Japanese words at his command, she ventured to answer: "I know; I give you the teach of Nippon, you give me the wise of dat funny 'Merican tongue."

"That's a go!" said Dick, as he held out his hand to close the bargain.

But the girl drew back, troubled.

"No, no, you no *go*! You stay. I give you all my intellect of Nippon speech. Please!" and she looked up pleadingly.

Merrit laughed outright.

"That's all right, Yuki San; I am going to stay, and we will begin school in the morning."

By this time the mother and father had learned of the guest's arrival and hurried in to bid him welcome. The unpacking of his steamer-trunk and the disposal of his possessions in his small apartment was a matter of interest to the whole family. Each article was politely examined and exclaimed over, and when Merrit drew out a package of photographs and showed them his home and family and friends, the excitement became intense.

That night Yuki San lay once more on her soft *futon* and watched the shadow of the night-lamp play upon the screens. Nothing was changed in the homely room since she had lain there in her babyhood: the same little lamp, the same little Buddha on the shelf looking at her with inscrutable eyes.

Yuki San stirred restlessly. "Dat most nice girl in picture," she said to herself. "Him make marry with dat girl, he say." Then she added inconsequently, with a sigh, "I much hope Saito San go to war for long, long time."

CHAPTER IV

For two halcyon months Yuki San lived in a dream. The ample compensation Merrit insisted upon making for the hospitality extended to him more than met the modest needs of the little household, and once again, as in the earlier days, they went on jolly excursions, visited ancient temples, and picnicked under the shadow of the *torii*. The father and mother always trotted close behind, and Yuki San, vastly pleased with her ability, gaily translated the speeches from one to another. She talked incessantly, laughing over her own mistakes, and growing prettier and more winsome every day.

Merrit was glad to fill his leisure time in such pleasant companionship. Yuki San was the same little bundle of charm he remembered of old, with her innocence untouched, and a heart whose depths had never yet been stirred.

He teased her, and taught her, and played with her, as he would have played with a merry child. Naturally gentle and affectionate, he unconsciously swept Yuki San to the borderland of that golden world where to awaken alone is agony.

One morning, when the heavy mists of the valley lay in masses of pink against the deeper purple of the mountain, and his Highness, the sun, his face flushed from his long climb, was sending his first glances over the sunny peaks of Fuji-yama, Yuki San arose, after a sleepless night, and faced the morning with sorrowful eyes.

"You ve'y lazy, Mister Sun, this morning," she said, shaking a finger at him in reproof; "where you the have been? Why you not come the more early and make light for my busy?"

She tied the long sleeves of her bright kimono out of her way, and twisting a bit of cloth about her head, fell to dusting the *shoji* and setting the small room in order.

"I must the hurry," she said, as she kept up her brisk dusting. "I make the food so quick as that Robin San steal berry for his babies. To-day him one big, big day, but him no glad day. Merrit San go away." She paused in her work, and a look of pain darkened her eyes, but she shook her head reproachfully.

"Ah, Yuki San, you make sorry voice and your heart is thinking tears. You naughty girl! Quick you make the fire to rise in *hibachi* and give that Merrit San his *gohan*—same thing what that funny 'Merica call breakfast."

After the steam had begun to rise from the vessels on several *hibachi*, Yuki San, flushed by her exertions, rested upon her heels before the door that led into the garden. As she fanned her flushed face with her sleeve, she glanced again and again toward the narrow stairway that led to the chamber above, and at the slightest sound she listened in smiling expectancy.

From outside the wall came the gentle slip-slap of the water against the *sampan*, and the cheerful banter of the owners as they made ready for the work of the day.

Circling the garden, the fern-like maples made a note of vivid crimson amid the feathery green of the bamboo. Every feature of the place was closely associated with her short happy life. She had learned to walk on the soft sandy paths, she had spelled out her first characters on the old stone-lantern. She had whispered her secrets to the broken- nosed image of Kwannon, who sat in the shadow of the pines, and there under the plum-tree she had caught the naughty kitten that first brought her and Merrit San together.

As she sat, with folded hands, and watched the sunshine on the dewy leaves and flowers, her intense, restless, vivacious body relaxed in sudden languor and her soft mouth drooped in wistfulness.

A splash in the pool below attracted her, and looking down she saw the gleaming bodies of the goldfish as they leaped into the air. Instantly she was all life and volubility.

"Yuki San one big bad girl; she no remember li'l fish. They always like hungry baby San in early morning. I make fast to fill big hole inside—ve'y li'l outside."

Slipping her half-stockinged feet out of her straw house-shoes, she stepped into her wooden *geta,* and passing a shelf, filled her hands with round rice-cakes.

The edge of the water turned to gold as the fish crowded close. Yuki San scattered the crumbs and stood watching the wriggling mass for a moment, then said:

"You ve'y greedy li'l fish. I never no can fill your bodies. Now I get flower for Merrit San's breakfast."

She made her way over the flat mossy stones, passed the miniature Fuji where dwelt the spirit of the wondrous "Lady who made the flowers to bloom." She paused before the gorgeous chrysanthemums and looked long at the morning-glories, with their tender tints of dawn. But at last she spied on a rose-bush, set apart from the rest, a single white rose with a heart of red.

With a little cry of satisfaction, she thrust her hands among the thorns to pluck it. The rebound of the bush sent fluttering to her feet a brilliant purple butterfly. Tender to all living things, Yuki San dropped quickly to her knees and folded the half-chilled creature between the palms of her warm hands.

"Ah, Cho Cho San," she said, "the day of yesterday you so big and strong. The morning of to-day you have the weakness of cold body. That Jack Floss him ve'y naughty boy!"

She put her moist red lips to her folded palms and the warmth of her breath stirred to action the gauzy creature she held captive.

"You no must kick, Cho Cho San! Have the patience. I make you warm, I give you one more day of happy."

Yuki San's wooden shoes sent a sharp click into the quiet morning air as she quickly crossed the arched bridge and followed the path to the stone image beyond the pool. With a touch as soft as the wings she held, the girl lightly balanced the now thoroughly warmed butterfly on the broad forehead of the Goddess of Mercy.

In sharp contrast to the spirit of the scene came the clear, rollicking strains of an American air, whistled by some one coming down the steps.

For a moment Yuki San stood motionless, pressing her lips softly to the rose she held. Then, with a swift pitter-patter, she ran back to the house.

"The top of the morning to the honorable Miss Snow," said Merrit, who quite filled the doorway.

Not willing to be surpassed in salutation, Yuki San laid a hand on each knee, and bending her back at right angles, replied with mock gravity:

"Ohayo Gozaimasu-Kyo wa yoi O tenki."

Merrit knew she had him at a disadvantage in her own language, but, always delighted to see the play of her dimples and the soft pink creep into her cheeks when he teased, he stood by her now, big and stern, and growling.

"See here, Yuki San, otherwise Miss Snow, you just come off your high stilts of that impossible lingo, and speak nice English suitable for a little boy like me to understand."

"Li'l boy like you!" she rippled, "li'l boy like you! Merrit San him so long when he make Japanese bow he come down from top like big bamboo-tree—so!" Putting her hands high above her head, she bent till the tips of her fingers touched the floor. Still bent, she twisted her head till her eyes, bright with laughter, looked straight into Merrit's.

He lifted his eyebrows quizzically. "See here, Yuki San, you are fast developing the symptoms of a coquette."

She quickly straightened her back, and with a smile of bewilderment, exclaimed:

"Me croquette? No, no; croquette, him li'l chicken-ball what you eat. I no can be eat!"

Merrit shouted with delight, then grew grave.

"No, Yuki San, you don't ever want to be a coquette. You want to be your sweet little self, and make a good wife to that handsome soldier Saito, with all his gold braid and dingle-dangles. But what about breakfast? You see, my train leaves in an hour. If you don't give me something to fill my honorable insides, I'll have to eat you, sure enough."

In mock fear she quickly brought a low table from an inner room, and with deft hands placed the steaming soup and broiled fish before him. The knife and fork were a concession to Merrit's inability to wield the chopsticks, and sitting on his heels was Merrit's concession to the inability of the house to provide a chair.

"Hello!" he said, picking up a long-stemmed rose, "where did you find this beauty?"

"I guessed her with my nose," the girl answered. "You know what make her heart so red? Long time ago, most beautiful princess love with wrong man. Make Buddha ve'y angly, and he turn her body into white rose. But her heart just stay all time red 'cause of beautiful love that was there."

"My! he's a fierce old customer, that Buddha of yours," said Merrit.

Yuki San paused in the filling of the rice-bowl and looked at him gravely:

"Merrit San, do you know God?"

"Do I know God?" he repeated, with a half-embarrassed laugh.

"Yes, Christians' God, what you must love and love, but no never can see till die-time come. You know, Merrit San?" Then, lowering her voice in earnest inquiry, she went on: "You believe that Christians' God more better for Japanese girl than Buddha?"

For a moment Merrit felt the hot blood of confusion rise to his temples. The role of spiritual adviser was a new and somewhat embarrassing one. Struggling for expression, he floundered hopelessly.

"I—I—I guess I don't know very much about it. But there's one sure tip, Yuki San, the Christians' God is all right. You can't lose out if you pin to him." He stammered like a foolish schoolboy, but struggled bravely on: "When things get pretty thick and you've struck bottom, that's the time you find out. I know. I've been there. More's the pity I don't remember it oftener!"

"And you think him more better for me?" asked Yuki San, still perplexed.

"You bet I do!" said Merrit with conviction. "Take my word for it and don't forget."

"I no forget," she said.

A sliding of the screen and a call from the court-yard announced the arrival of the jinrikisha men, who had come for the baggage.

Merrit thrust back his half-finished breakfast.

"By Jove! I'd most forgotten this is my last meal with you. Just to think all that tiresome old government contract is finished and I'll soon be on my way to the other side!"

"You want to see other side?" she asked. "Mama San not there no more." Then seeing his face darken, she laid a quick hand of sympathy on his. "I have the sorrowful for you," she said earnestly, then went on hastily: "That other side! Yes, I know that most beautiful 'Merica. Most big ship in the world come rolling into Hatoba. Merrit San so long and big, stand way out front and see over much people. Then he cry out, 'Herro!' herro!' with glad and much joyful. He see that lovely girl like picture waiting there!"

Without pausing for a reply, she pushed open a door and called in Japanese to her father and mother, who never made their appearance till Merrit's breakfast was finished.

"Come, make ready to give our guest an honorable departure," she said.

In the small courtyard facing the street the girl found the men, with their jinrikishas and baggage-wagon, waiting to convey Merrit to the station. She carefully directed the tying on of the various trunks and bags, and placed the family just where they should stand that the greatest honor might be done the departing guest.

As Merrit came out of the little house and reached for his shoes, which stood waiting at the side, Yuki San started toward him, eager to serve him to the last. Merrit motioned her back.

"Don't come too near, Yuki San. If you happened to fall into one of those shoes, you'd be lost for ever and ever, and that big Mr. Saito would be inviting me to cut off my head."

Yuki San laughed and smoothed the cushions in the jinrikisha while she gave minute directions to the jinrikisha men.

Merrit made his adieu with high good humor, and so many big words that Yuki San was hard pressed to interpret. He invited the family and all their relatives to come to see him in America. When he reached Yuki San he held out his hand. Made shy by the unusual ceremony, she timidly laid a cold and unresponsive little palm in his. He looked down from his height with tender memories of all her gentle courtesies.

"Good-by, little snow-girl," he said. "I'll never forget Japan, nor you."

She withdrew her hand and looked inquiringly up at him.

"Some long time you come back?"

Merrit climbed into the jinrikisha "No, Yuki San, you know I'll soon have a little home of my own to work and care for. I'll be a busy man for the next few years, so I guess I'll not come back."

As in a dream, Yuki San saw the men adjust their hats and tighten their sashes as they took their places in front of the small vehicle. Mechanically she bowed her farewell with the rest of the family, but she did not join their "Sayonara."

She watched the swift moving of the jinrikisha wheels, then she saw Merrit turn at the gate and wave his hat as he joyously called:

"Good-by, Yuki San, God bless you!"

The girl stood still, her eyes on the empty gate. Like a lonely, hurt child her lip quivered, and she caught it between her teeth to steady it.

"Ah, Yuki," cried her mother, "some spirit has wished you harm. A drop of blood rests on your lips."

Yuki San drew her hand across her mouth, and lightly answered that maybe a robin had tried to steal a cherry. But to herself she murmured:

"My heart bleed for lonely. He *never* come back."

CHAPTER V

The following day a host of accumulated duties and various preparations for the first ceremonious visit of the groom-elect kept Yuki San's hands and mind busy, and if sometimes a sob rose in her throat, or her eyes strayed wistfully from her task, she resolutely refused to let herself dwell upon the past.

The marriage, which had been dutifully accepted as a matter of course and looked forward to as a financial relief to the entire family, had never held any particular interest for her, but now even the preparations, which had hitherto excited her interest and enthusiasm, found her listless and indifferent.

She would be mistress over a great mansion and many servants, and her days were to be spent in arranging for the physical comfort of Saito and the entertainment of his friends.

The arrangement had seemed so simple, and so right, and she had been gratified that a desirable husband had been found. But now she could neither understand nor explain to herself her new and strange resistance. She only knew that for the first time in her life there was rebellion against the inevitable.

As she rested her tired body before beginning her toilet for the afternoon, she remembered an American teacher at school who had been *in love* with the man she was soon to marry. She remembered how she had hidden behind the trees to see this young teacher run to the gate to meet the postman, and her own failure to see why these letters should bring such joy. She, with other girls, had spent a whole recess acting this scene amid peals of laughter. Now it all came back to her with new meaning, and it seemed neither strange nor amusing.

She leaned her head against the open *shoji* and looked out into the garden, radiant and beautiful in the high noon of a perfect autumn day.

The working world paused in a brief sleep and the music of the garden was hushed, while the insects sought the shadow of green leaves. Peace was within and without, save in the girl's awakening heart.

"Ah, Sensei," she murmured through her trembling lips. "Then I make fun for your letter of love. Forgive my impolite. Now I the understanding have."

Yuki San chose her toilet for the coming visit with due regard for all convention. There must be no touch of purple—that being the color soonest to fade made it an evil omen. She selected an *obi* of rare brocade, the betrothal gift of Saito, the great length of which expressed the hope of an enduring marriage.

As she dressed, her mother flitted about her, chatting volubly and in such high spirits that Yuki San's heart was warmed. The elaborate trousseau had caused the little household many a sacrifice, but the joy in the hearts of the old people more than justified them.

Presently the clatter of the jinrikisha in the courtyard announced the arrival of the guest. Yuki San heard the long ceremonious greeting of her father. She saw her mother hasten away to do her part and, left alone, she sat with troubled eyes and drooping head.

The strange feeling in her heart, one moment of joy and one of pain, bewildered and frightened her. No thought of evading her duty crossed her mind, but her whole being cried out for a beautiful something she had just found, but which it was futile to hope for in her new life.

At the call of her mother, Yuki San silently pushed open the screen and made her low and graceful greeting. Custom forbidding her to take part in the conversation, she busied herself with serving the tea, listening while Saito San recounted various incidents of the picturesque court-life, or told of adventures in the recent war.

After all the prescribed topics had been discussed and the farewells had been said, Yuki San retained a vague impression of a small, middle-aged man, with many medals on his breast, who looked at her with kind, unsmiling eyes.

It was not till after the simple evening meal that Yuki San found the chance to slip away to the little upper room which had been Merrit's for two months. Nothing there had been touched, for the old mother claimed that to set a room in order too soon after a guest's departure was to sweep out all luck with him.

The girl entered and stood, a ghostly image, in the soft and tender light of the great autumn moon as it lay against the paper doors and filled the tiny room. Through the half-light Yuki San saw many touches of the late inmate's personality. A discarded tie hung limply from a hook on the wall, a half-smoked cigar and a faded white rose lay side by side on the low table.

From the garden the sad call of a night-bird, with its oft-repeated wail, seemed to voice her loneliness, and with a sob she sank upon her knees beside the cot. Long she lay in an abandonment of grief, beating futile wings against the bars of fate. At last, throwing out her arms, she touched a small object beneath the pillow. Drawing it toward her, she took it to the open *shoji*, and by the bright moonlight she saw a small morocco note-book. She puzzled over the strange figures on the first few pages, but from the small pocket on the back cover she drew forth a picture that neither confused nor surprised. It was the girl Merrit had told her about—the girl to whom he was going so joyously.

It was a face full of the gladness of life and love, whose laughing eyes looked straight into Yuki San's with such a challenge of friendship and good will that the girl smiled back at the picture and laid it gently against her warm cheek.

She sought out each detail of hair and dress as she held it for closer inspection, then replacing it in the pocket she said softly:

"He have the big, big love for you. You give him the happy. I close my heart about you."

On the back of the book in letters of gold she spelled out the strange word, "Diary." She puzzled for a moment, then she remembered where she had seen it before. The young American teacher had written in just such a book, and when she asked its meaning, the teacher had said it was her best friend, her confidant, to whom she told her secrets.

For a moment Yuki San stood with the book in her hand, then she said impulsively:

"Diary! I make diary, too. I speak my thoughts to you. I tole you all my secrets. Maybe my lonely heart will flew away."

CHAPTER VI

THE DIARY OF YUKI SAN
First Entry

'Merican Sensei say she have one closest friend in little book. I tell my troublesome to this little book what spells "Diary" in gold letters on back. I make it my closest friend what no never speaks the words of yours when heart overflows with several feelings. I write for Merrit San, but his eyes no must never see. Just my heart speak to his heart in that 'Merican tongue what he understands.

Japanese girl very naughty if she love man. She made for the take care of man's mother, man's house. Very bad for Japanese girl to say love when she marry with man. Merrit San say 'Merican girl speak love with eyes when lips are shame. Japanese girl cover the eye with little curtain when man comes. She no must peep out one little corner. No must see, no must hear, no must speak the love.

So I make little book guess my heart each day.

The happy days are pass away, and the flowers are bloom and birds will return to me again, but where can I find Merrit San? How I feel the sorry and the lonesome when I think I can't find him no more in this long island. I no can express my heart with words. I never the forget of his kindness to me.

Big lamp by Merrit San's desk no never burn so bright for me. It make funny little crooked shadow of my body on *shoji*. Merrit San's body always make big and strong black picture. I saw it last time big moon look over mountain. I took walk in garden and I thinking this time next moon Merrit San will not be here. Though the lamplight shines through the *shoji*, still in next month the owner of the light will be different and the ache come into my heart.

Whole Japan are changed, and everything I see or hear makes me think of him; but my thoughts of him never, never changed, yet more and more increase and longing for him all time. My heart speak the much word of love for Merrit San. My eyes grow shame to say it. Little book, close my secret!

Second Entry

ALL day many rains come down in garden. He steals flowers' sweetness and damp my heart with lonesome. Last rainy day Merrit San teached me more better English, and he laugh very long when I read the English writing with my Japanese tongue. He say: "Ah, Yuki San, you very funny little girl!"

Then I teach him the play of *go ban*, and he make the pain in his head with the several thoughts how he must move the black or white. He try long, long time, then he shake his big feest, and he say: "You've got me beat, little sister; you've got me sure."

I laugh, but I think much thoughts. *I* no hurt Merrit San with beat, and girl with much laugh in her eyes have got him for surely. I no understand that funny 'Merican tongue.

Merrit San so many time call me little sister, and he say my soul all white like my name. What *is* my soul? Ah, that same spirit what leave my body and go out 'cross that many seas to safe Merrit San's journey. I keep that soul all purely and white all of because Merrit San call me Little Sister Snow.

One day I take Merrit San with me to very old temple. Sun, him so bright he make all leaves to dance with glad. Green lizard take sleep on stone step while big honey-bee sing song. All things have the joyful, and my feets just touch earth with lightsome.

I go inside temple and say one very little pray to Amida, for I have the hurry. When I go back, Merrit San he say:

"See here, Yuki San, you no waste time over pray. You get the trouble with that old gentleman if you have not the careful."

Then I say: "Next time I give him little money and make big smoke with incense," and he say, "Yuki, you very good girl."

Just by temple's side is little bamboo-tree which have very nice story. One good god he like this bamboo, and he like the beautiful love. He say give names of man and woman to boughs of bamboo and make the tie together with long pin of thorn. Give the low bow, and by and by the dear wish in heart will be truly.

Merrit San he no can know what I do, but he hold the high boughs of bamboo down and I name him and me and make the tie together.

The dear wish of my heart come not truly. It is full of sad.

Third Entry

What shall I do to less my anxious? To-day at temple I ask Buddha. He never speak. He always look far away at big sea. He no care, though tears of the heart make damp the kimono sleeve. The Christians' God I no can see. But Merrit San say he is everywhere and listens for voice of troublesome. I no can make him hear, though I say the loud prayer.

Buddha very ugly old god. Maybe him cross when he see very pretty Japanese girl make the low bow to him.

I believe Christians' God more better than Buddha, because Merrit San say he make everything truly. He make me, he make Merrit San, he make the beautiful love. Maybe some day that big God hear about Japanese girl's heart of trouble and speak the peace.

To-day one long so busy day. Many silk must be sewed into fine kimono for the when I go to live in other house. Sometimes I very glad I go to other house. I make the many comforts of my mother and my father.

To-day I see the much cold in my father's body. Very soon he have nice warm kimono with sheep's fur all inside. Then I make the glad heart, I marry with Japanese man.

It is getting little cold, and every night the moon is so clear. These day crickets are singing among the grasses. Those make me to think of Merrit San more and more. This fall was quite changed to me. At first Merrit San never come back to me as I expect in dreamy way. I have the feel of very helpless and lonesome. Before, though I had some trouble or unhappiness, if

I saw Merrit San's smile everything was taken clear away and my heart was full with cheer and happy.

Ah, Merrit San, though it makes my cheek red with hot to write the speak, I love you most.

Buddha very naughty old god to say nothing truly is.

Fourth Entry

Ah, Merrit San, what you suppose I have dream last night? I was so happy that I cannot tell with my tongue nor pen. That *you* come back! I could no word speak out with so much glad. I had many things to tell you before I wake, but I could not even one thing.

You say you stay ten days. It is too short, but it far more better is than half night. Oh, I wish so bad I did not wake up from dream!

I was tearful with much disappoint, then I remember that day you go to big 'Merica you call back "God bless you, Yuki San," and with my heart I make one soft prayer to Christians' God.

When big temple bell wake me up and all birds, my troublesome was more light, and I make so big breakfast for my father and my mother, my pocket began to tell the loneliness, and I could not perform all my wishes.

When I write these letters Merrit San is far away at sea on the way of his home. He will have joyful time. I wish I can see her, that girl with the laugh in her eyes. Wonder how she thinks of Japan. Perhaps she would think how small and lonely country and people. One girl in that Japanese country very sad with lonely.

But Merrit San say: "Yuki San, you *good girl*, you be good wife." So I make the try to put my lonely heart to sleep.

Fifth Entry

Time and days goes too fast as running water. Already old month went away and new one have come. It is time for us to do last work on many clothes for new home.

When Japanese girl marry with man she take much goods to his house. To-day my father bring what 'Merican call bureau, and many work-box and trays and much fine *futon* for to sleep on floor with. Next day after this many mens will come and travel all things to other house. Japanese girl wear fine kimono long, long time, and keep for more little girl. Merrit San say 'Merican girl wear fine kimono one time, then she no more like.

Then 'Merican girl have much happy in her heart. 'Merican man come to girl's house to marry with her. She no afraid to speak the word of love, though man's mother sit next by him. She no 'fraid of laugh. She has the joyful of life.

Japanese girl very happy when she very little girl, or very, very old. But when she goes to man's house to marry with him, she must always be the quiet of little mice and more busy than honey-bee. Very bad. But Japanese girl have the much brave, and holds the happy in her heart when she brings the comforts to her peoples.

Merrit San say many more big country than Japan in world. I say, "What is world? I wish I know world like you!" Merrit San stop the laugh and his voice grow still with quiet, then he say:

"Ah, Yuki San, little snow-girl like you should not know the world. Cuddle in your little nest and be content."

What is content? It is the don't care of anything but the flower- garden in my heart. Wonder if girl with laugh in her eyes have the content? This day I take walk by seas. Last time I take walk so many peoples come with us. I make into Japanese words all Merrit San's funny speaks. We have the much laugh: Merrit San try the eat with chop-sticks.

To-day little boat what we ride the water in was broke by its nose and many seas was eating it up. Loud cold wind make pine-trees shivery and sad. Big gray cloud come down and make all black with sorrowful. Sometimes little white waves jump up and dance, but the joyful of last happy day stings my heart.

Sixth Entry

More long time go running slowly by since you have left us, and as I was thinking of that running and those days and longing for you and my heart getting down in lonely thoughts, *Yubin* San bring me those package what you sent, Merrit San, and it made me very glad and happy. Hardly can I tell what was in my heart then. Before I can open it I hold it tightly against my breast and kept silence a little while. Tears of sorrow changed into the great joy for a moment when I see your name and your hand of write. I feel as if I receive a new life right in this minute, and I caught a light of hope in yonder. My heartful joy and gladness will not express, and I wish I can go up in high place and shout out and tell all people the joyful of beautiful love. How it make the change in whole earth and life and give the dance of heart. But I will not. Mens and women of Japanese country have not the understand of such lovely thing, and make the shameful of me. So I give silence to my lips and close the door of my heart. Ah, what funny little thing that heart is! In one half live the joyful. Other side have all the painful of life, and when the love come sometimes he knock at wrong door and give the hurtful ache to life. Ah, Merrit San, you give many thankfuls for the lend of my house in your letter. I give the love of you many more thankfuls for coming to my heart, even he knock at two doors. One day me and Merrit San went down to temple where big feast was. Merrit San go inside and look long long time at Buddha, then he say:

"Yuki San, what will this old gentleman do to you if you disobey him?" I give little think, then I say, "I no can know—I no never disobey. Buddha say, 'Yuki, take care father and mother all time.' I take care. Him say, 'Yuki, you woman—you not talk too much.' I no talk much. Then him say, 'Yuki, come many time to temple and make light with incense and put little money every time in box.' I give obey and much *go rin*, but Buddha keep all and never give back." Before I finish my speak Merrit San shiver like cold and say, "Come on, Yuki San, let's get out of here and find the sun." Outside I make cherry-wreath while Merrit San tell me story. Him very sweet day—now all gone forever.

Seventh Entry

Last fine kimono is finished and all baggage is tied. Next day I go to other house.

Then my mother will give all house much sweep with new broom, to tell gods I go 'way no more to come back. Maybe they make big fire by gate to tell all peoples I belong to other house now. Ah, little book, to-night I make big fire in my heart and burn all my wickeds in it. Next day I make more fire and burn you. To other house I must go all white and purely as Merrit San say.

Ah, Merrit San, you the one big happy in all my life and I never forget all your kindful. You give me the good heart, like sun make flower-bud unclose. You told me what is soul and purely, and you say be very good wife.

One night when moon was big and round and red and river outside wall go spank, spank, you call all my people to garden, and with the 'Merican *samisen* you sing much songs.

Sometimes you very funny, but sometimes when moon specks slip through big pine-tree, I see you very sadful.

Now moon speck come on *shoji* and ache my eyes to look your face once more.

I try so much to make picture of man's face I marry with. I no can see anything but much medals on coat, and so many teeths. Merrit San's eyes all blue and twinkly, and face so white and clean.

But now he make the joyful with girl with laugh in her eyes, and her feet no touch the ground with much happy.

To-morrow I go to other house and no belong to my father and mother. To-day I go temple, and I make promise I no more speak of Merrit San's name; no more the think of his face in my heart.

Little book, I weared you close to my breast many days. To-night I sleep with you tight to my heart. You gived me the courage to turn my face to the rising sun of the to-morrow.

Sayonara.

CHAPTER VII

The low, deep music of a temple bell rolled down the hillside and echoed through the giant cryptomerias. It stirred to action the creatures of the early dawn and passed out with infinite sweetness to the red-rimmed east of another day.

The priests in the old temples chanted their prayers with weird monotony, while a single bird poured out his morning song of love at the door of his mate.

The old stone steps leading from temple to temple would have looked as they had a thousand other mornings, gray, grim, and mossy, save for a little figure that slowly took its way up a long and crooked flight.

Yuki San was on her way to make good her promise to the gods. Her wooden shoes clicked sharply in the quiet morning air, then hushed as she paused for rest on a broad step. Even the exertion of the long climb had failed to color her white cheeks, but her lips were carmine and her eyes luminous with purpose.

The one spot of color about her otherwise sober little figure was a bright-red *furoshike* held close, in which something was carefully wrapped.

A noisy waterfall leaped past her down the hillside in a perpetual challenge to race to the foot. Stern-faced images, grim of aspect, stared at her as she climbed, but Yuki San kept gravely on her way until she reached the open door of the great silent temple.

The faint light of the early morning had scarce penetrated the shadows that clung about the gorgeous hangings and rich symbols of this ancient place of worship. A white-robed priest, oblivious to all save his own meditations, paid little heed to the childlike figure as it knelt before the cold, calm, unchanging image of the great Buddha.

For a moment Yuki San moved her lips. Still kneeling, she drew from her sash the red *furoshike* and took from it a small morocco note- book.

With light steps she crossed to a brazier, and with a pair of small tongs lifted from it a glowing coal. With steady fingers she pushed aside the many sticks of incense in the great brass vessel before the shrine, and making a little grave among the ashes, she laid within the burning coal the little book.

The blue smoke, rising slowly, hung for a moment above the girl's head as a halo, then rose to the feet of Buddha as in supplication for mercy, and was finally lost in the darkness of the heavy roof.

The girl watched with wide eyes and parted lips. Clasping her hands, she lifted her face and from her heart came a fervent, whispered prayer.

"I make empty my heart of all wicked. Buddha or Christians' God, I no can know which. Please the more better speak into my lonely life the word of peace."

She turned from the silent temple on her homeward way. She paused by the clump of bamboo where so short a time before she had gleefully tied together two boughs in the name of Merrit and herself. Tiptoeing to reach the high boughs which Merrit had held for her to tie, she drew them downward to slip the thong that bound them. After holding them to her soft cheek a moment, she let them fly apart, while she closed her eyes and whispered softly:

"Good-by, beautiful love, good-by."

O02887831
FICTION LIT
Little, Frances,
Little Sister Snow,

DUNHAM PUBLIC LIBRARY
76 Main St
Whitesboro, NY 13492
(315) 736-9734

7/2020